Tokyo Friends
Tokyo no Tomodachi

TUTTLE PUBLISHING
Tokyo • Rutland, Vermont • Singapore

Also by Betty Reynolds
Clueless in Tokyo

This book is dedicated to my nephews and nieces,
Joseph, Jennifer, John Stanley, Jessica,
Ian, Veronica, Juliana, and Caitlan
and to all of my
chiisai Tokyo no tomodachi

Published by Tuttle Publishing, an imprint of Periplus Editions
(HK) Ltd, with editorial offices at 364 innovation Drive,
North Clarendon, VT 05759 USA and 61 Tai Seng Avenue
#02-12 Singapore 534167

© 1998 by Periplus Editions (HK) Ltd.
All rights reserved

LCC Card No. 98-87067
ISBN 978-4-8053-1075-5

First edition, 1998

13 12 11 10 09
12 11 10 9 8 7

Printed in Malaysia

TUTTLE PUBLISHING® is a registered trademark of Tuttle
Publishing, a division of Periplus Editions (HK) Ltd.

Distributed by:

Japan

Tuttle Publishing
Yaekari Building, 3rd Floor
5-4-12 Osaki, Shinagawa-ku
Tokyo 141-0032
Tel: (81) 3 5437 0171; Fax: (81) 3 5437 0755
Email: tuttle-sales@gol.com

North America,
Latin America &
Europe

Tuttle Publishing
364 Innovation Drive
North Clarendon, VT 05759-9436
Tel: 1 (802) 773 8930; Fax: 1 (802) 773 6993
Email: info@tuttlepublishing.com
Website: www.tuttlepublishing.com

Asia Pacific

Berkeley Books Pte. Ltd.
61 Tai Seng Avenue #02-12
Singapore 534167
Tel: (65) 6280 1330; Fax: (65) 6280 6290
Email: inquiries@periplus.com.sg
Website: www.periplus.com

You are lucky if you live
in Tokyo today.
You can do things the western
or Japanese way.

Although Japan may be different
than where you come from
learning a new culture
can be so much fun!

Tokyo,
Japan

おんなのこ
onna-no-ko
girl

アメリカじん
Amerikajin
an American

あう
au
meet

いぬ
inu
dog

Tokyo friends are easy to meet. Say "hello" or

きょうだい
kyōdai
sibling

おとこのこ
OTOKO-no-ko
boy

にほんじん
Nihon jin
a·Japanese

じてんしゃ
jitensha
bicycle

"konnichi-wa" when you see them on the street.

あくしゅする
akushu suru
shake hands

ともだち
tomodachi
friend

You can shake hands in greeting or learn how to bow.

おじぎをする
ojigi o suru
bow

Katie, Keiko and Kenji will show you how.

ワッフル
waffuru
waffle

めだまやきとハム
medama yaki to hamu
eggs and ham

シリアル
shiriaru
cereal

ミルク
miruku
milk

オレンジジュース
orenji jūsu
orange juice

あさごはん
asa gohan
breakfast

ナイフ
naifu
knife

スプーン
supūn
spoon

フォーク
fōku
fork

パンケーキとベーコン
pankeki to bekon
pancakes and bacon

You can eat a western breakfast or one Japanese.

のり **nori** *seaweed*

おちゃ **ocha** *green tea*

サラダ **sarada** *salad*

おしぼり **oshibori** *moist hand towel*

つけもの **tsukemono** *pickles*

なまたまご **nama tamago** *raw egg*

sakana さかな *fish*

ごはん **gohan** *boiled rice*

みそしる **miso shiru** *soybean soup*

なっとう **natto** *soy beans*

hashi はし *chopsticks*

Use a fork or hashi, whichever you please.

うんてんしゅ
untenshu
driver

バス
basu
bus

のる
noru
ride

あるく
aruku
walk

Kenji walks, while Katie rides the bus to school.

えびす

でんしゃ
densha
train

えき
eki
train station

Keiko's train is very crowded as a rule.

バックパック
bakku-pakku
backpack

スニーカー
suniika
sneaker

えんぴつ
empitsu
pencil

けしごむ
keshi gomu
eraser

しょうがくせい
shogakusei
primary school student

Aa Bb Cc Dd Ee Ff Gg Hh

Some books are read from left to right,

あいうえおかきく さしすせ

せんせい
Sensei
Teacher

ランドセル
randoseru
knapsack

うわばき
uwabaki
inside shoes

はさみ
hasami
scissors

つくえ
tsukue
desk

クレヨン
kureyon
Crayon

others right to left-to.

You may buy your lunch...

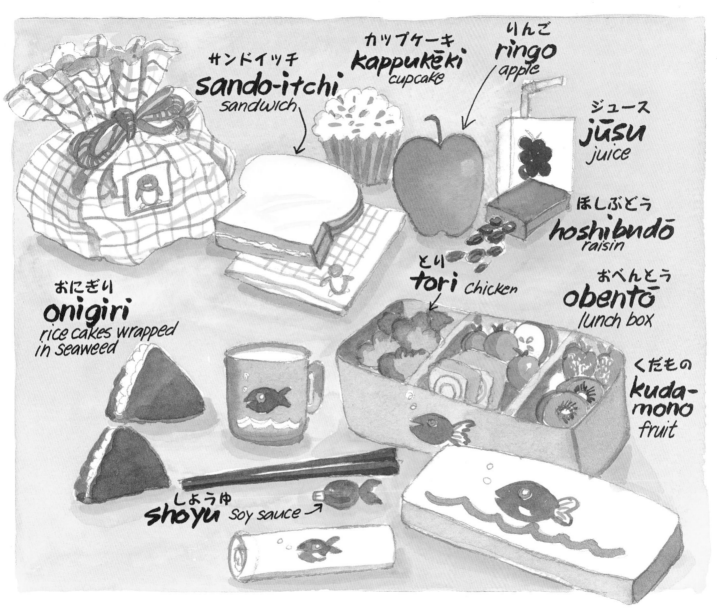

カップケーキ
kappukēki
cupcake

りんご
ringo
apple

サンドイッチ
sando-itchi
sandwich

ジュース
jūsu
juice

ほしぶどう
hoshibudō
raisin

とり
tori *chicken*

おべんとう
obentō
lunch box

おにぎり
onigiri
rice cakes wrapped in seaweed

くだもの
kuda-mono
fruit

しょうゆ
shoyu *soy sauce* →

or pack an obentō.

いち
ichi

に
ni

さん
san

し
shi

こ
go

一二三四五六七八九十

You can fold your fingers in to count...or unfold them

out. Either way, you get to five...without any doubt.

レストラン
resutoran
restaurant

ウエイター
weitā
waiter

ばんごはん
ban gohan
dinner

MENU
ピーサ
スパブ
サラダ
コーヒ

You can eat at a table with chairs...

のれん
noren
curtain

かぞく
kazoku
family

むすめ
Musume
Daughter

おとうさん
otō-san
Father

ざぶとん
zabuton
pillow

たべる
taberu
eat

or sit on cushions on the floor. Sometimes you

おかあさん
Okā-san
Mother

りょうりてん
ryōri-ten
restaurant

くつした
kutsushita
SOCKS

くつ
kutsu
shoes

...must leave your shoes inside the front door.

Some noodles you shouldn't slurp. Some noodles

そば **soba** buckwheat noodles

you may. Spaghetti is a no-no but soba is okay.

In a western bath you can have soap in the tub but no water on the floor.

かがみ
kagami
mirror

タオル
taoru
towel

ハブラシ
ha-burashi
tooth brush

せんめんき
semmenki
sink

あわ
awa
bubble

Take a morning bubble bath or use the ofuro at night.

In a Japanese bath you can have water on the floor but no soap in the tub.

ふろば
furoba
bathroom

シャワー
shawā
shower

シャンプー
shampū
Shampoo

てぬぐい
tenugui
hand towel

おふろ
ofuro
bathtub

おけ
oke
Wooden bucket

But scrub outside the tub first if you want to get it right.

Some friends sleep on a futon. Some, on a bed

ベッド
beddo
bed

ゆめ
yume
dream
↓

にんぎょう
ningyō
doll

ほんばこ
hon-bako
bookcase
↓

ほん
hon
book
→

ねこ
neko
cat

that's tall. But when they get together...

ねまき
nemaki
pajamas

まくら
makura
pillow

はね
hane
feather ↗

あそぶ
asobu
play

they hardly sleep at all!

There are many things
to see and do
in Tokyo
the whole year through.

And quite a few
will be new
to you.

ふゆ
Fuyu
Winter

はる
Haru
Spring

なつ
Natsu
Summer

あき
Aki
Fall

かどまつ
kadomatsu
A new year
decoration
that wards
off evil

しめかざり
shimekazari
An offering to the
gods for a good
harvest

かがみもち
**Kagami
mochi**
Pounded
rice cakes
representing
the sacred
mirror

いちがつ
Ichigatsu
January

かしわで
kashiwade
Worshippers clap their
hands and ring the bell
to get the gods attention.

There are 10 full days of New Year cheer.

はごいた
Hagoita
A paddle used in a childrens' game

だるま
Daruma
A doll to make a wish on

はまや
Hamaya
A good luck charm

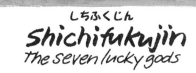

しちふくじん
Shichifukujin
the seven lucky gods

Stand in line to ring the bell or buy a souvenir.

にがつ
Nigatsu
February

February's Setsubun can be fun when you

おにはそと
"Oni wa soto"
"Out with the devil"

ふくはうち
"Fuku wa uchi"
"In with good luck"

Setsubun せつぶん

The day before the first day of Spring.

Roasted soybeans are thrown to ward off evil and bring in good luck.

It is considered good luck to eat the same number of beans as your age.

throw beans at demons to make them run.

だいりびな
dairi-bina
The Emperor and Empress →

さんにんかんじょ
sannin-kanjo
ladies-in-waiting →

ごにんばやし
gonin-bayashi
Court musicians →

Ministers of the right and the left. →

three attendants →

court furnishings →

さんがつ
sangatsu
March

Girls' Day in March is called Hina Matsuri

さくらもち
Sakura-mochi
sweets wrapped in
cherry blossom leaves.

ひなまつり
Hina Matsuri
On March 3rd, families
display Hina dolls to
give thanks for their
daughters' good health.

when dolls are displayed in all of their glory.

ちょうちん
chōchin
lantern

うたう
utau
sing

Katie, Keiko and Kenji sing off-key at

さくら
sakura
cherry blossom

しがつ
shigatsu
April

a flower-viewing party called hana-mi.

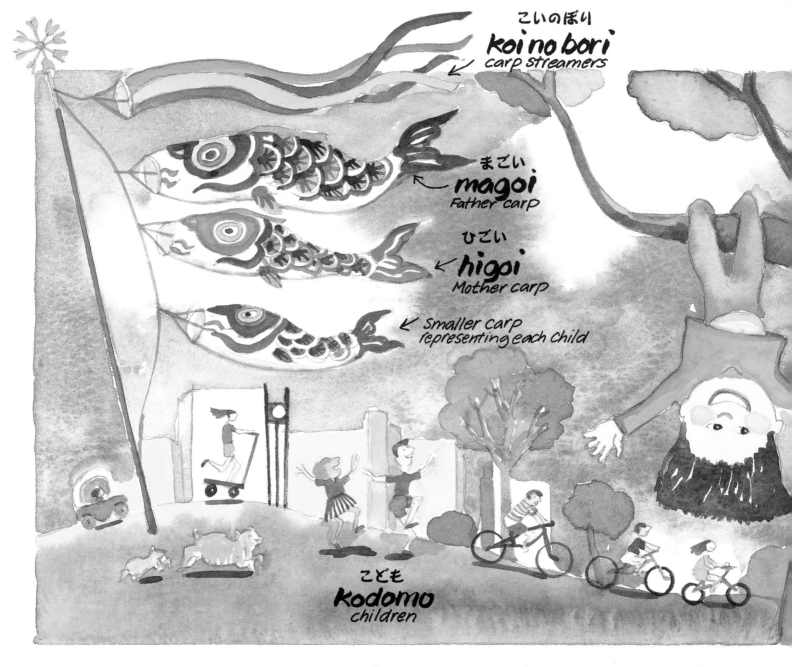

こいのぼり
koi no bori
carp streamers

まごい
magoi
Father carp

ひごい
higoi
Mother carp

↙ *smaller carp representing each child*

こども
kodomo
children

In May the children are filled with glee on

ちまき
Chimaki
Rice dumplings wrapped in bamboo

かしわもち
kashiwa mochi

Sweet rice wrapped in oak leaves

ごがつにんぎょう
Gogatsu ningyo
Minature Samurai armor

こどものひ
Kodomo no hi
Children's Day

Many years ago May 5th was called Boys' Day. Now it is a national holiday for all children.

ごがつ
Gogatsu
May

their own special day called Kodomo no hi.

こぶね
kobune
boat

みずうみ
mizuumi
lake

Riding a boat in June is a lark on

a tiny lake in Inokashira park.

From June through July it's the rainy season time.

あめ
ame
rain

はし
hashi
bridge

みずたまり
mizu-tamari
puddle

Kids like to splash in every puddle that they can find.

たなばた
Tanabata

Poems are written on colored strips of paper and hung on bamboo branches during the Tanabata festival.

うちわ
uchiwa
summer fan

ふうりん
fūrin
wind chime

しちがつ
shichigatsu
July

かわ
kawa
river

In July there are fireworks called hana

はなび
hanabi
fireworks

わたがし
wata-gashi
cotton candy

かきごおり
kakigōri
shaved ice with syrup

アイスクリーム
aisu-kurimu
ice cream

やきもち
yaki-mochi
pounded rice balls dipped in soy sauce

bi which all of Tokyo goes to see.

やぐら
yagura
festival platform

In summer time you'll have the chance to

ちょうちん
chōchin
lantern

ゆかた
yukata
cotton kimono

おぼん
Bon Festival
Bon music and dancing welcome the ancestors' spirits back to their native homes.

たこやき
tako-yaki
small cakes with octopus

やきそば
yaki-soba

fried seasonal noodles and vegetables

おこのみやき
Okonomi-yaki
Japanese pizza

ラムネ
ramune
popular childrens' beverage

wear a yukata and do the O-bon dance.

In August you can join the community

はちまき
hachi-maki
headband

まつり
matsuri
festival

おおだいこ
ō-daiko
large drum

by taking part in a local matsuri.

You can watch sumo wrestlers go toe-to-toe

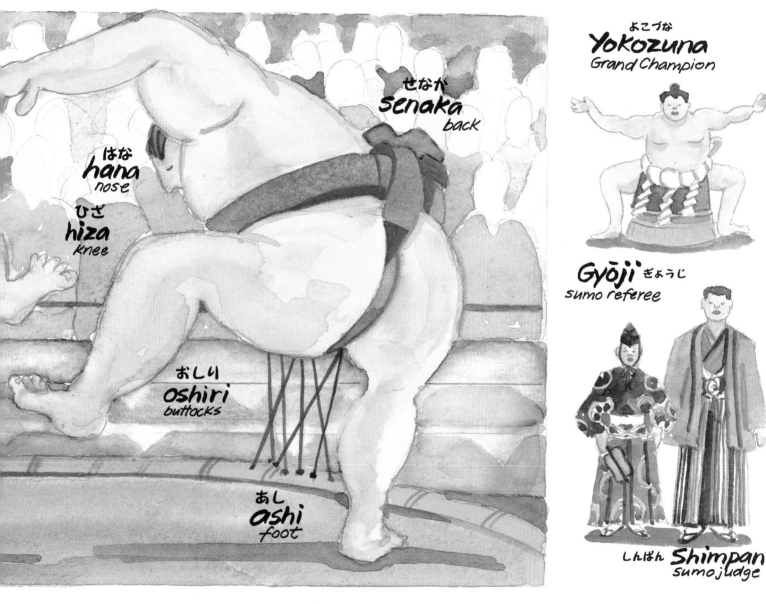

せなか
senaka
back

はな
hana
nose

ひざ
hiza
knee

おしり
oshiri
buttocks

あし
ashi
foot

よこづな
Yokozuna
Grand Champion

Gyōji ぎょうじ
sumo referee

しんばん **Shimpan**
sumo judge

at the September tournament in Tokyo.

こうよう
kōyō
autumn leaves

シェーキーズ

KIDDY LAND

Jūgatsu じゅうがつ
October

Omotesando has a kids' parade for Halloween

じゅうだいのしょうねんしょうじょ
jū-dai no shōnen-shōjo
teenager

みせ
mise
store

but dressing up is more fun when you are a teen.

じゅういちがつ
Jūichigatsu
November

ふりそで
furisode
long-sleeved kimono

はおり
haori
short coat

はかま
hakama
pleated skirt

しゃしん
shashin
photograph

ぞうり
zōri
slippers

Shichi-go-san is for children aged seven, five and three.

おび
obi
sash

ちとせあめ
chitose-ame
"A thousand years
of happiness candy"

Three-and five-year-old boys
and three-and seven-year old
girls are taken to a local
shrine on November 15th
to insure good health
and happiness.

People take their photo and give them candy for free.

クリスマスカード
Kurisumasu kādo
Christmas card

okurimono
おくりもの
gift

クッキー
kukkī
cookie

しちめんちょう
Shichimenchō
turkey

ハヌカ
Hannukah

Candles are lit during this Jewish holiday

はしご
hashigo
ladder

December is filled with holiday fun.

ゆき
yuki
snow

じゅうにがつ
Jūnigatsu
December

ねんがじょう
nen ga jō
New Year's card

おせいぼ
o-sēbo
year-end
gift
giving

もちつき
mochitsuki
The pounding
of rice to
make mochi

おもちゃのでんしゃ
omocha-no-densha
toy train

としこしそば
toshikoshi soba
traditional New
Year's eve meal

There's a family tradition for everyone.

だいぶつ
Daibutsu
Big Buddha

はと
hato
pigeon

Taking a train to Kamakura is fun any time. You

くも
kumo
cloud

そら
sora
sky

でんしゃ
densha
train

き
ki
tree

きっぷ
kippu
ticket

はとサブレ
hato-sabure
pigeon-shaped cookie

can visit the Big Buddha and temples and shrines.

When each and every day is done Tokyo Friends
are tuckered from all their fun.

The next day, bright and early, they'll be out the door because there is always something new to explore.

Sayonara!

Goodbye till we see you in Tokyo.